1000
STEPS

1000 STEPS

W. NEWTON REID

1000 Steps
Published by W. Newton Reid
New Zealand

© 2025 W. Newton Reid

ISBN 978-0-473-75662-8 (Softcover)
ISBN 978-0-473-75663-5 (ePUB)
ISBN 978-0-473-75664-2 (Kindle)

Production & Typesetting:
Castle Publishing Services
www.castlepublishing.co.nz

Cover Design:
Quinn West

I'm at the bottom of the steps, looking up, wondering what's next...

The stormy wind and troubled sky echo exactly how I'm feeling.

I'm upset. More than sad. I'm gutted.

Feeling wretched and isolated

and alone.

It's not that I'm an emotional teenage girl,

or overwrought.

I'm not being overly dramatic.

I've just had a rough time of it recently.

I've usually got an optimistic, positive disposition.

But not now.

Tears keep showing up unannounced.

My heart is aching.

Grieving for what might have been.

I look up at the steps stretching before me,

wondering what is next.

The steps lead to the top of the cliff.

The place known as 'Lover's Leap',

for all the jilted lovers over the years.

Lovers who have thrown themselves

onto the rocks and sea below.

And I guess other people who are suffering.

A permanent solution to the

temporary problems life hands them.

The sign doesn't say that though.

It just says, '1000 steps to the lookout.'

A thousand steps.

Is it really?

I've been here heaps of times,

but I've never counted all the steps before.

Never questioned the written words.

I started counting steps as a child.

Even now at nineteen, I still do it.

Check to see how many there are.

Like the counting police.

One thousand steps – that's a lot of climbing and counting.

I look down, shuffle my feet and stare at the gravel,

rooted to the spot,

procrastinating.

My pain feels familiar.

It takes me back to one of my first memories.

It's like I'm four all over again.

My mind drifts.

Uncle Sid is scary.

His husky voice makes a hacking kind of laugh.

It turns into a cough.

A hand-rolled fag hangs from his lips.

It bobs up and down,

raining ash over his always dirty shirt

    and whatever else is close.

        He doesn't seem to notice.

His hands are rough, and his fingers are cracked and hard.

Deep lines cover his tanned face.

Once I saw him eat a triangle dog biscuit.

    His big black dog is scary too.

Another time he chased my little brother

    with a freshly caught trout.

    It was gaping with large, glazed eyes.

      Sean was only two.

        He thought it was going to eat him.

        Screaming he ran to me.

I glared at Uncle Sid.

He just hacked a laugh that dropped ash on the trout.

He's my mother's uncle.

We see him a lot.

He lives alone.

His wife left.

We're visiting Grandad.

Uncle Sid is there too.

I try to avoid him.

Today I'm not fast enough.

His strong hands grab me.

He's looming over my four-year-old frame,

poking,

tickling.

I shrink into myself with each unwanted touch.

I'm not ticklish.

I'm not giggling.

I wince and wriggle to get away.

Wanting him to stop.

Trying to escape,

but he keeps on.

Finally, he smirks and releases me,

but it's only to play monster.

He grabs me again.

He wants me to run.

To run so he can catch me and win.

He's strong and grabs my soft flesh.

It crushes me.

It hurts.

I feel sick.

I think I'm going to wet my pants.

I look at my mother.

She glances over with a slight frown as she knits.

Click, clack, click.

She doesn't read my terror.

She doesn't say anything.

I stare at his cracked, yellowed fingers holding me,

and surrender.

I can't win.

Too scared to run.

I lean away from his foul breath, and look down at the

flowers on Grandma's carpet.

He moves in closer.

Hovering just above my head,

as I cower from his slobbery lips,

helpless and mute.

Red and pink flowers, faded carpet, old carpet.

He's in control.

Mum's knitting is important.

Clack, click, clack.

Her lips have gone thin.

I wonder what to do.

I'm not a cry-baby,

or a squealer.

A good girl right here.

Glancing directly at Uncle Sid,

willing him to stop.

Trying to figure out how to get him to end this torture.

What words to use.

My brain has frozen.

I don't dare say STOP, or NO.

'No' is a bad word for a child.

That's what I'm told.

I need a grown up to save me.

Finally, I find my voice.

'Mummy, can I play outside?' I plead.

All eyes move to me.

I feel my face heat up.

'Please, *may* I play outside?' I correct myself.

'No, stay here where I can see you.'

She doesn't lift her head.

At last Uncle Sid releases me.

I scurry to my mother's side.

'I'm going to the bog.'

He glares at me as he stalks off.

'That wasn't nice,' my mother whispers.

'He was just playing.'

My eyes brim.

I hang my head and hold my tummy.

I don't look at anyone,

only at the different coloured flowers on the carpet.

I focus on crossing my arms and legs,

to make myself small.

I want to be invisible.

My mother frowns and looks down at me.

I look up hopefully.

'Best behaviour when we visit Grandad,'

she admonishes quietly.

The heat returns to my upturned face.

I hug my legs and bury my head on my knees.

I want to go home,

where I feel safe.

I sit quietly next to my mother instead.

I feel bad in so many ways.

It's a grown-up world.

Children should be seen and not heard.

There's tension in the air.

Mum puts her knitting down.

She looks at everyone and no one.

'So, as I was saying before I was *rudely* interrupted,'

she continues.

She glances at me.

'I've decided to leave James.'

I don't get it.

Where is she going to leave Daddy?

Grandma sighs.

Grandad frowns and narrows his eyes.

'Is that necessary?'

'Yes,' she replies, raising her chin.

'I've had enough.'

Grandma looks at me sadly.

My tummy feels like spiderwebs.

'It'll be easier to nurse Mum and take care of things,

so you can keep working.

I'll move with the kids into the small bedroom.'

I look around at the silent grown-ups.

Everyone seems to know what it's all about.

I don't.

She picks up her knitting again.

'We'll move just before Christmas. Won't that be nice.'

She says it to no one in particular.

I look up at my mother.

She doesn't see the confused frown.

She's forgotten about me.

I'm invisible after all.

Just like a child should be.

The car is ready to leave but I'm not.

Daddy is still at work.

Mr Hagley has loaded the packed stuff onto the trailer.

I thought Mr Hagley was Daddy's friend.

I stand at my bedroom doorway,

while sadness surrounds me

like an overpowering, grey cloud.

'Why can't I sleep here anymore?'

'Because we're moving in with Grandad and Grandma.'

'But what about Daddy?'

'He's staying here.'

'Are we coming back?'

'No. Now get in the truck and be quiet.'

This feels all wrong.

Daddy's going to be upset when he gets home.

When he reads the note on the table

and sees we're gone.

It makes me squirm, but I do as I'm told.

Like a good girl.

I don't understand grown-ups.

I don't understand why we're leaving.

We're supposed to be a family.

Mummy, Daddy, me, and Sean.

Now Daddy's not one of us.

The three of us share a single room.

Mum in a bed on the left.

Sean and I in a bunk on the right.

There's a foot space in between.

Just enough to walk between

and close enough to jump from the top bunk to the bed.

If we were allowed.

By the time Mum comes to bed, we're already fast asleep.

Me being only four.

Sean only two.

When we moved in.

One small bedroom out of three.

Two boarders in another.

Grandad, Grandma, and Ryan crammed in the third.

Their 'adopted' son and now my big brother.

Older than me by only a year and a half.

He's the favourite.

He bosses me around like he owns everything.

He's got two mothers in the same house now.

The first grandchild.

That's when I first feel hate.

I hate that I've lost my place.

I used to be the oldest.

I hate him bossing me around.

But here we all are, a new kind of family.

Making the best of it.

There's no room for Daddy.

Not in Mummy's heart either.

I wonder if he's lonely,

and who makes his dinner.

Maybe he's forgotten about us.

The toilet is outside at Grandad's house.

It's a long walk in the middle of the night.

I try not to think about what else might be

sharing the dark space,

as I creep past the shadows.

Flushing makes a

loud, scary sound

in the quiet night air.

It's better to hold on until it's light outside.

The big vegetable garden next to the shingle drive

makes good mudpies.

Salt the slugs but save the slaters.

Washing flapping on the line.

Chooks clucking in the henhouse.

Mine was black and plump.

We ate it for dinner.

I like it here though.

Grandad, Grandma, Ryan,

Mum, me and Sean

And the two boarders.

We've arrived at Uncle Sid's house.

'There's no one else to look after you,' Mum says.

I stand wide-eyed at Uncle Sid's back door,

    clutching Sean's tiny hand.

The paint is peeling off the wood on the doorstep.

    A spider is eating a fly in its web in the corner.

'Be a good girl and do as you're told.'

Uncle Sid opens the door.

    A fag in the corner of his mouth.

      We're pushed up onto the cracked lino.

'They've been fed and it's nearly bedtime,' she says.

'Don't worry,' he splutters with his

    wonky cigarette dropping ash.

    'There's the pellet machine.'

We know about guns.

We've been to the gun club lots of times now.

    Uncle Sid and Grandad shoot rabbits and ducks too.

      Uncle Sid makes his own bullets to save money.

We watch and listen.

The pellets rattle around and around.

Sean holds onto me tighter and tighter.

The machine is much bigger than us. It jiggles and roars.

The noise hurts our ears.

The house smells funny,

like oil, cigarettes, and old man.

It's messy and dirty too.

Finally, we crawl into the couch bed.

I rub Sean's back to soothe him.

He's afraid and wants Mummy.

He finally falls asleep next to me.

I do too until Uncle Sid's heavy hand rests on my shoulder.

It wakes me.

He rolls me over.

I open my eyes a little,

still groggy.

Awake enough to be worried.

He's undone the flap of his old man's stripy pyjama pants.

Snakes start squirming in my tummy.

I look away,

at my brother peacefully sleeping.

I don't want to see.

Don't want to touch it.

Don't want to hear.

To smell.

Don't.   want.   to.

Horrible, bad man.

Don't want to.

No cry-baby here.

Mum picks us up the next morning.

    Tears lurk around my eyes, but I'm no cry-baby.

I hang my head as we leave,

    and mumble the thank you.

'That was nice of Uncle to have you over, wasn't it?' she says.

My head nods, mouth muted.

'Did he show you the pellet machine?'

'Yes,' Sean piped up with bright eyes, 'it was noisy.

I saw his gun.'

Mum looked at me.

'Would you like to stay again?'

'No,' I croaked, head still down.

'That's not very nice,' she says.

I'm shaking inside.

    Squirmy and anxious.

        Children don't tell tales on grown-ups.

When we get home, I don't feel like playing.

    Just climbing up to my bed,

        and curling into a tiny ball.

I hold the punishment for your crime.

Vulnerable,

    naïve,

        innocent.

Trapped with a criminal.

No one teaches you how to deal with this kind of stuff.

Especially if you're a good girl.

                              It's overwhelming.

I only know how I feel,

                              and it's bad.

You were supposed to protect me.

    To keep me safe.

      You're a bad man.

        You've done bad things.

I can't make sense of it.

    I only know how I feel.

      I don't want to remember it.

I shake myself out of the haze.

How long have I been standing at the bottom of the steps?

Procrastinating.

Remembering.

My eyes trace the steps up.

They're still rising before me like an invitation.

One that my legs are reluctant to accept.

My brain wills them to move.

Wisps of hair blow into puffy eyes.

Hands sweating.

They're little steps.

At least if I'm counting,

I'm not overthinking and

analysing.

I won't have to listen,

to the devil on my shoulder

taunting me,

feeding me with

a damaged inner monologue

stripping away the good.

If I'm counting, I won't have to suffer the bad memories,

that keep dropping in uninvited.

The bad memories can disappear,

and leave me alone.

Perhaps they will if my mind is otherwise occupied.

I don't have the energy for this climb,

but I want to reach the end.

I want peace.

Besides, I'm here now.

I've decided.

So, I must go through with it.

At least I can check if it really is a thousand steps.

Maybe it's only nine-hundred-and-ninety-nine.

If it is, I could tell someone they got it wrong.

That I figured it out.

I'll focus on the steps,

and nothing else.

I can control that.

I want to feel in control somehow.

I take the first step.

Grandma's bed is in the lounge now,

so that she can see what's going on.

She's waiting for the cancer to claim her.

I know she's sick,

because we must be quiet.

Especially if she's sleeping.

I try to make her happy.

'You're a good girl,' she says.

'You wouldn't say bum for a dollar.'

I don't know what that means.

Who'd offer me a dollar to say bum?

Bum is a silly word, a bad word.

I wouldn't say a bad word, no matter what.

I sit quietly. I don't know the words to explain my feelings.

They're everything – large and consuming.

Grandma is still watching me.

'She's been here before,' she says to Mum.

'Got an old soul.

You can see it in her eyes.'

Mum squints at me.

I squirm.

I do feel old sometimes.

My words are too small for these big feelings,
I just sit quietly.

I'm not ready when it happens.

A big black shiny car

crunching on the gravel.

It stops outside our bedroom.

Grandma is dead.

I won't ever see her anymore.

'Be quiet and stay in your room with Sean,' Mum says.

'Why can't I come and see?' I beg.

'Because children DO AS THEY'RE TOLD!'

She slams the door.

I sit wide-eyed and fidgeting on the threadbare carpet,

desperate to be included.

To have it all explained.

Who are the strangers in our house?

Where are they taking Grandma?

Why can't I come out and say goodbye?

I hang my head and rub my eyes.

It's not fair.

Sean is zooming his cars on the floor, making silly noises.

I climb up on Mum's bed,

and peer between the slats of the white venetian blinds.

It's hard to see anything.

I know Mum will be cross if I bend them.

The blinds are always hard to handle.

Pull the cord hard and they go up but don't stay up.

Or they end up all wonky.

High on one side and low on the other.

It doesn't matter how carefully I pull them,

they never do what I want.

They inch their way back down

towards the windowsill,

one painful tug at a time.

Or they drop too quickly,

and land with a crash

and get me in trouble.

I can't risk pulling the blinds, so I peer through them,

hoping to see or hear something.

I can't.

I just want to know what's happening. To understand.

The big black shiny car backs out the shingle drive.

That's the end of that.

Grandma is gone now too.

I still have Sean.

I don't want to lose him.

It's nice sharing a room and keeping him close.

The bunk wobbles when I climb up to the top.

We make our own fun.

Sometimes Sean has trouble getting to sleep,

so I help him.

Tick tock tick tock –

I hang my hand down like the arm of a clock.

Back and forward, swing the arm,

focus on the arm Sean,

go to sleep, go to sleep.

Don't worry, I'm here.

He grabs my hand and licks it.

'Eeew, Sean!' I squeak, wiping my hand on the old,

pink candlewick bedspread.

'I got you then!' he laughs, delighted at himself.

'Very funny,' I say. 'How about I tell you a made-up story?'

Now I'm a schoolgirl, I can make up stories.

He falls asleep in the middle of this one.

Soon after, I do too.

We carry on like this, happy in spurts.

Comrades in our little room.

I want to protect him from bad things.

Like the bad thing that had happened to me.

It's cold in winter.

My feet get freezing,

 with frosts and an old damp, draughty house.

At night I do a full circle

 under the covers.

  It warms me and the bed,

   before I drift off to sleep.

If I'm cold, I can't sleep for shivering otherwise.

  Even with my hair over my ears they're cold.

  My feet moan until I rub them together,

   or do the undercover swim.

Tonight, I fall asleep half-way.

  My head under the covers

   at the foot of the bed.

    My feet on the pillow.

I wake later, struggling to breathe.

My head is pinned down in a tightly tucked-in cocoon.

  Smothered.

   Panic overtakes me.

Terrified and disoriented, the dark is overwhelming.

The tightness holds me.

I wrestle against the cloth restraints,

sweat across my red face,

gasping.

Helpless.

My scream is a muffled sound that goes nowhere.

I turn left and bang against the wall.

To the right I hit the bar.

Panicking

screaming

struggling.

I can't escape.

I can't breathe.

Suddenly, the cloth loosens as one side is untucked,

and the covers thrown back.

Wide-eyed and tear-stained I take great big gulps of cold air.

'What on earth are you doing?' Mum whispers.

'I fell ... asleep ... halfway,' I sob, trying to gain control.

'Shh, your brother's sleeping.'

'I got stuck ... couldn't breathe,' I whisper.

'Well, you're out now, so be quiet about it.'

She snickers as if my fear is hilarious.

'Can I stay up with you?'

'No, go back to sleep like a good girl.'

I take a deep breath and make myself strong.

My feet are cold.

At the breakfast table it was a funny story.

But not to me.

'I could hear this screaming, but it seemed far away,'

Mum laughs.

'No wonder, with her head tucked in at the end of the bed,'

Grandad said.

'It's a wonder she could breathe.'

'Next time you'll fall asleep the proper way,' Mum said.

The proper way.

The proper way.

I

never

did

an

undercover

swim

again,   just in case.

My thoughts won't shut up.

I remember counting forty-nine steps,

but the memories have interrupted my counting.

Am I at fifty or sixty?

My count is messed up now.

I can't be certain if I'm correct at all.

There's no point continuing the count if it's all screwed up.

I could go back down and start again,

but it's not that important to know.

It won't make a big difference.

Besides – I don't have the energy.

Getting to the top is the point.

Focusing on numbers didn't stop my thoughts from tumbling,

one over the other after all.

I sigh and look up.

Still nine-hundred-and-fifty or so,

if there really was one thousand to begin with.

Ten steps later there's a new plan.

I'll let the thoughts come.

I'll just divert them by thinking about something else.

If they're controlled,

they can't cause chaos.

I don't want to pick the scab,

regurgitate the event,

or dwell on the negative bits of my past.

I can be intentional with my thoughts.

I can do that.

I used to have the same nightmare over and over.

It was about getting lost in a building with lots of corridors,

with a bad man chasing me.

Halfway through the dream I would go blind

and then listen to him getting closer

and closer to me,

while I huddled, helpless in a doorway,

unable to see, unable to run.

The dream always ended as he grabbed me.

I always woke up afraid.

I wrote the dream down like a story and changed the ending.

Instead of the bad man catching me,

a nice man rescued me.

A strong, kind man picked me up

held me in his arms, and my sight returned.

He protected me and showed me

the way out.

Saying to me, 'Everything will be ok.'

I read it over and over.

The next time I had the dream, the nice ending happened.

I woke up feeling that everything WOULD be ok.

I never had that nightmare again,

but I wanted to find that nice man.

Now I long for a nice man to hold me.

To tell me everything will be ok.

I know I can't write away my memories.

Even in my mind they change through time.

Perhaps if I acknowledge them as part of me,

But not all of me.

The past, but not the present, or the future.

I can stop them from overwhelming me.

I can rewrite the ending to something good.

I can be more.

There's so much I can't control.

Like the way others behave.

Like bad memories.

Like the weather.

The wind blows my hair and my clothes around.

The clouds build and move across the sky.

Control is an illusion.

All I can control is me.

We have a lot of good times

at Grandad's.

Long days in the country

while Grandad is hunting or fishing.

I love climbing tall pine trees – rough bark and sticky sap,

getting to the top and seeing far away,

feeling the scrape of the branches,

the smell of pine,

the sway of the tree.

Carting heavy rocks to make dams in cold rivers.

With slimy beds that make you slip

and get bruises.

Leg badges, reminders in

black, blue, then green.

Picnics in golden grass.

Campfires that make our clothes smell after.

Squishing sandflies.

Coming home to the smell of a roast.

Watching a Disney movie,

tummies rumbling,

eyelids drooping.

Simple fun that makes me laugh and smile.

Loving the country outings.

For ages, Mum bikes us everywhere.

At the 'Gardens' we love to climb the rocks,

    visit the playground,

        splash in the shallow pool with a grey whale

        in the middle.

        It spouts water.

Spring flowers, green grass, beautiful trees

        and a river with ducks to feed.

        I sit on the wire back carrier of the bike.

            Sean sits on a special front seat.

I love feeling the wind in my hair,

        the push of her legs,

            the surge that follows each pedal,

peeking out the side to see where we're going,

        bouncing up,

            then back hard on the wire rack when

        we go over a bump.

My six-year-old legs get tired,

as I cling onto the seat for a long ride.

        We go over a bump.

I bounce up then back onto the hard seat

and don't hold my leg out.

My errant foot goes into the back wheel.

We all come off.

I scream and scream at the throbbing pain.

People come running to get my foot out of the spokes.

I can't help but cry this time.

It hurts so bad we go home.

When Mum gets a car, we can go further.

We're out past our bedtime.

Changing into pyjamas in the back seat.

A race to see who's first.

Falling asleep on the ride home.

Magically waking up in bed the next morning.

We become like a family again. Grandad and Mum

and us three kids.

Happy and together with our own rhythms

and routines.

Porridge in winter with cream sometimes in the morning.

Scratching Grandad's socked feet until my fingers hurt,

at the end of his hard day

while we wait for dinner.

I always look out for Sean.

He needs it with all his crying and naughtiness.

Now he's in for the strap.

'Right, I've had enough of you,' Mum says.

She grabs the long piece of tyre rubber.

'No, please don't hit him,' I beg.

'I won't do it again,' Sean says wide-eyed.

'That's what you said last time.'

She grabs his wrist and raises the strap.

He starts running.

They spin around each other, like a funny show.

She swats at him.

I raise my hand to pull her arm, and the blow hits me.

I cry out.

'That's what you get for not minding your own business,'
Mum says.

Sean pauses when I yell, and the strap connects

with his bottom next.

He cries and runs to hide in the toilet.

Alone in his brief misery.

A lock on the door.

My other brother is watching from the kitchen.

'Now you know what it feels like,' he says.

They call me 'goody two shoes' because I do as I'm told.

That's why I don't get the strap.

At school, I watch out for Sean and even my older brother.

If they're picked on, I tell the other kids off.

I'm not scared of them.

Today there's a drama at school.

A puffing teacher comes to get me in class.

'You have to come,' she insists, wide-eyed.

I hurry after the teacher along the corridor,

    and outside to the school pool.

Sean is screaming and clinging to the bar of the steps

into the pool.

    The rest of the class bob at the other end,

        trying not to look but wanting to.

        He's beside himself with terror.

A teacher is leaning over him,

        trying to pry his hands off the bar.

            His face is red from screaming and clinging.

'He won't stop screaming,' the teacher explains.

I hurry over to him and wrap my arms

around his shivering body,

    glaring at the teacher.

    Sean stops screaming and clings to me.

        Then he glares at her too.

    She steps back.

Then,

    she walks away:

        hands up and shrugging,

            as if she's done nothing wrong.

Slowly Sean's colour returns to normal,

    from red to pink to paler than usual.

      A sob escapes.

'She was trying to make me!'

    He sobs again. 'I don't want to.'

I wish I could scream like Sean when I don't like stuff.

    Scream like I did on the bike when my foot got jammed.

      Lots of people came to help me.

If I'm scared, I don't scream.

    I don't fight.

      I don't run.

        I freeze.

          My brain and my mouth stop working.

Wrapping a towel around Sean, I help him out,

    then stand guard at the changing room door

    while he gets dressed.

This is my place.

I'm his big sister.

I'll be there for him no matter what.

We sit together on the grass,

not talking while the rest of his class gets changed.

Finally, I look over at him.

He's hunched beside me picking at the grass

next to the concrete step.

I can tell he's embarrassed and humiliated and angry,

and relieved I'm there.

'Why didn't you want to get in?' I ask.

'She was going to push my head under,' Sean said.

'I saw her do it to the others without even asking.'

Sean likes the water,

but he's terrified of his head going under.

I've never thought about God.

Until today.

A girl at school is boasting about memorising

the Lord's Prayer.

'What's that?' I ask.

'You don't know the Lord's Prayer?'

I frown at her for putting me down like that.

Does she think she's smarter than me?

I'm not stupid.

No one knows everything, anyway.

'Never heard of it,' I say.

She mumbles a whole lot of words unfamiliar to me.

'I can't understand what you're saying,' I say.

'I need the words written down.'

At eight, I'm already reading big chapter books.

If she can memorise something, I can too.

I want to memorise it faster than her,

so that she doesn't put me down again.

'Come to church with me and you can get a copy,' she says.

I don't know why she just doesn't write it down for me.

I want a copy, and Mum let me go with her.

That's when I made up my mind about God.

It's not like I haven't been to church before.

Everyone's been to weddings and funerals.

It's just that God isn't talked about at home.

Not acknowledged or discussed or known about.

No embroidered scriptures on the walls.

We don't even say grace.

I didn't know anything about God.

Never thought about it.

I knew deep down that someone big

must have made everything.

Someone bigger than the whole world.

Someone clever.

I hadn't thought about him making me though.

Or what he thought about me.

I'm sitting on the mat with a bunch of other kids.

'God is everywhere,' the Sunday School teacher says.

'You can talk to him out loud or in your head anytime.'

That's convenient since I often want someone to talk to.

'He knows everything,' she says.

I like that too. I want to know as much as possible.

'We're all his children. He'll never leave you.'

I like that as well. I don't want to be left.

'He's made a home in heaven for you because he loves you.

To get there you must believe Jesus came to save you.'

I don't know what I need saving from.

'He died on the cross to take your punishment.'

I've always tried to be a good girl,

I wonder what I've done wrong,

that needs punishing, I mean.

'Accept him, live by his rules and you'll see him

in heaven one day.'

I'm wondering what his rules are since I follow

a lot of rules already.

'What if we don't?' a smartie-pants pipes up.

'We make our own hell,' the teacher says and shudders.

That shut him up.

The teacher went on.

'There is good and evil everywhere,

even at war inside us,

so choose wisely.

Choose life.'

That's a lot to think about, especially the choosing.

I think about it, but not that long.

The answer seems obvious to me.

If God is real and all those things are true,

then he's powerful.

That makes him a bit scary,

and it makes sense to keep him happy.

Plus, I want someone that's always around

to talk to.

When I die, I want to go to a nice, safe place.

If God is not real and none of it is true, then

nothing will happen when I die.

There'll just be nothing.

At least I would've lived with a code

and believed in something

bigger than me.

I make up my mind to keep God on my side.

The God that created everything, even me.

It seems like the only sensible thing to do.

I memorise the prayer and tell that girl from school.

I make a promise to myself to try to please God

from now on.

I tell Mum too.

She says now I'm a goody-two-shoes Christian.

I'm not allowed to look down on her.

As if I would.

I'm not even as tall as her yet.

I'm excited.

About being a bridesmaid for Mum's wedding, I mean.

She's excited about Morris.

I'm not so sure.

I like our family, and I don't want to change it again.

Sometimes he gives me the heebie geebies.

It's strange calling him Dad when I already have one.

Even though I hardly see him.

Perhaps I'm not that important to him.

I think he's forgotten about me.

My hair has been done all fancy by a hairdresser.

It's a grown-up style piled on top of my head

with flowers and everything.

I've even got a long dress even though I'm only

eight and a half.

We all move away from Grandad.

I wonder if he's lonely now that we're gone.

Who will make his dinner?

Now he's got all the rooms to himself

at the old house.

Now there's a new school,

a new two-storey house with a pink bedroom

all to myself.

I've got a new kind of family too.

Mum, Morris, me, Sean, and Ryan.

Ryan came with us.

I heard the grown-ups talking about it.

When I was sneaking around trying to

find out stuff.

I like to know as much as possible.

Grandad said Ryan needs his mother.

It makes sense.

I don't know where I fit anymore.

Again.

My two brothers play together with cars and silliness.

They leave me out.

I'm only a girl after all.

It turns out being a girl is not so good.

In more ways than one.

Playground bullies.

At the playground I can happily play by myself.

On the swing or climbing things.

Making tunnels in the sand.

Today is not so peaceful.

A boy about my age is pushing around a little girl.

He's pulling her hair and her clothes.

She's trying to get away.

She can't.

She looks scared and about to cry.

It's not right to pick on someone like that.

I yell at him, 'Leave her alone!'

I want to help her. Protect her.

He stops and glares at me.

So she runs away while he's distracted.

I'm happy for her

and walk towards the gate to leave too.

That's when two big boys grab me.

They drag me to the wire fence behind a shed.

They pin me there.

'Think you're better than us?' one says.

'Who says you can tell us what to do?'

'You're just a skinny white girl,' says another.

'You can't do anything.'

'You can't even save yourself.'

The first one turns to the boy I told off.

'We'll hold her, and you can hit her,' he says.

The boy darts his eyes left and right.

I struggle to get away.

The boys are stronger than me,

holding me each side.

It isn't fair.

'If you keep moving, we'll make it worse,'

the second one says.

I stand still, annoyed at myself.

I'm not the type to yell and scream

or act like a wild animal.

I wouldn't be able to win against them anyway.

I'll have to take it.

I ask God to help me.

Maybe I can duck at the last minute.

That's when the punch hits my tummy.

The other two giggle.

'Don't muck around with her stomach,' the first one says.

'Hit her face.'

My eyes widen.

The boy looks at me wide-eyed too.

He's taking his time about it.

Squinting, looking away.

He doesn't want to.

I hope he refuses to hit a girl in the face.

I hope he stands up for what's right.

That's what a good boy would do.

'Get on with it,' the older boy growls at him.

There's no conviction in his second punch.

I take it, frozen to the spot, chin raised.

I'm not going to cry.

'You can hit harder than that,' one of them says.

I close my eyes.

I pray the next one doesn't hurt.

That's when they let me go.

I open my eyes and see them running off.

The little girl is back, and she's brought her big brother.

He's much older than them.

I slump with relief.

She nods at my tentative smile, and they escort me home,

without a word.

The next day at school she finds me.

'Thanks for helping,' she says.

She shyly hands me a gold cross before

scampering off.

I clutch that little cross with Jesus on it.

It's proof.

God was listening,

to both of us.

Puffing fills my ears.

I don't even know how many steps I've gone.

It's got to be at least a couple of hundred.

I'm puffing,

> but that doesn't mean anything.

I don't like climbing steps, even little ones.

There must be a good reason for it.

> I've got a reason

> – to get to the top.

> I still don't like climbing steps.

They should put markers every hundred to let you know

how many.

> Unless they haven't really counted them.

It'd be much easier to count between markers of a hundred

to check.

All I know is I'm further along than I was before.

> It's a competition with myself now.

> Reaching the top.

I dread Uncle Sid visiting.

He's come for dinner.

He wants me to sit on his knee.

Again.

I turn towards Mum.

'I don't want to,' I whisper.

I glance at him wide-eyed, then back at Mum,

willing her to understand.

'Can I please just sit here with you?'

I move closer to Mum for protection,

hoping she'll figure it out.

'Do as you're told,' Mum says. 'It won't kill you

to be affectionate.'

I stiffen and hang my head,

hurt at the accusation.

Resigned.

Heavy legs walk over to Uncle Sid and sit on the edge

of his knee.

He lifts me back, right against his tummy.

He holds me tight with one hand,

and moves my dressing gown to hide his other hand.

What he does hurts.

He keeps talking with Mum

as I squirm to get away or make him stop.

Mum gives me a stern look that tells me to stop wriggling.

Uncle Sid pushes me away.

'You don't like hugs, do you?' he says.

I'm angry at his words,

and what he did.

'May I please go to bed now?' I ask.

Mum nods, and I scurry upstairs to my sanctuary.

It's not even bedtime.

I curl up into a ball under the covers,

staring blankly.

Not seeing the wall, begging sleep to come.

Asking God what to do.

Wondering if God will help me.

Uncle Sid doesn't visit again.

I don't know why.

I'm just glad of it.

I pray for a girl.

Mum is pregnant.

I pray as often as I think about it, that it will be a girl.

    Wishing wells get my coins for a girl.

I long for a little sister.

    Someone to be close with

        even though I'll be nearly ten by the time

        she's born.

If it's a girl, we'll grow up to be best friends.

    I'm sure of it.

Potential boys' names taunt me.

    Hopefully it's not a boy.

        It's only fair that it's a girl.

The two boys can keep their cars and planes and
stupid games.

We can do better stuff together.

    Two girls who understand each other.

        I'll be her big sister and protect her.

        It must be a girl.

It's a girl.

Three months before my tenth birthday,

my

little

sister

is born.

Big smile on my face.

    I can hardly wait for Mum to come home with the baby.

Morris says I can sleep in the big bed,

    on Mum's side

        because it's warmer than my bed.

The smell of her on the pillow is comforting.

I've never been allowed to sleep in the big bed before.

    I feel special as I drift off to sleep,

        thinking about my baby sister.

I wake in the night to tugging on my pyjama pants.

    It's dark and not time to get dressed.

    'It's my job to teach you how to be a woman,'

        he says.

    I don't want to be a woman.

I just want to be a little girl.

I want to sleep and see my new baby sister and my mother.

I wish I was in my own bed, even if it's cold.

I feel confused and sick. But mostly confused.

My tummy is full of snakes.

I close my eyes and pretend it's not happening.

Then I'm in my own bed again, shaking.

I think it's from the cold but I'm not sure.

I don't speak of it, don't even want to think about it.

That would make it more real.

I want to pretend it didn't happen.

The baby is a girl.

That's all that matters right now.

My bike is freedom.

I got it for my tenth birthday.

Riding it up and down the street for ages

pumping my legs,

focussing on the movement.

I'm in control of the bike.

I can make it do what I want.

Go where I want.

I'm alone and free.

Biking and listening to my transistor radio is the best.

My transistor radio that I bought with my own savings.

Even though I'm only ten.

The music fills my mind.

I love listening to all the parts of it.

All I feel is the push on the pedals,

the wind in my hair,

and the sounds.

Something bad has happened.

The body knows what the mind does not yet grasp,

    and it remembers.

I don't understand, I can't comprehend,

    but I feel sick inside.

I FEEL all wrong.

    I have no words to explain it,

just a sense that something bad has happened to me,

    And there's no one to help.

        I focus on other stuff but the bad hangs around.

I can fly.

    It's the best dream.

    Standing on my bedroom windowsill

    with the window wide open.

    It's dark but I can see way down the street.

    Powerlines and streetlights

        and the hills in the distance.

            I love the view of the hills and the mountains.

    It's not cold – it's not anything.

        The breeze lightly tickles my face,

           and moves my long fine hair.

           Inviting me.

    I spread my arms and lean out.

        I take a step, and overbalance...

    Air rushes past me as I leave the ledge.

        Not falling but flying.

           Under and over the power lines and then higher.

           Nothing restrains or controls me.

    Freedom to go where I want.

    I head for the trees.

Laughing and flying in the dark sky.

I'm part of the world,

the air,

the night.

The stars smile at me. The breeze whispers to me.

I'm joined with the gently moving trees.

One with nature.

They are me and I am them.

No one can see or touch me.

I am spirit.

Connected with the land, the sky, the universe.

When I wake, I pray to have the dream again.

I make it come as often as I can.

I need a rest.

At five hundred steps there's a worn wooden chair.

Whoever built it must know –

this is the place that legs get wobbly.

I plonk myself down and rub my thighs,

until my breathing is normal again.

There's a good view.

It's beautiful, storm clouds and all.

Creation is no accident from chaos.

Not at all.

Cabbage trees, ferns and flax are everywhere.

The wind makes them dance.

Birds sing and fly around.

If I was a bird, there'd be less to think about.

Finding worms and flying.

Feeling the air and using the breeze.

Free to go wherever.

I stare at the steps ahead and stand.

I can't sit here forever and it's already been a while.

I've got somewhere to be.

A new place, a new nightmare.

We leave the two-storey house with my own room
when I'm ten,

and move to a brand-new house in a new town.

My old friends are gone.

I hardly got to know them anyway.

The boys have a bedroom together.

I share one with my baby sister.

When she cries in the night I leap up and rock her
back to sleep.

This is my place now.

I hug her close and feel connected.

She smiles at me and relaxes.

I protect her and look after her.

My brothers are different siblings.

'I'm going to get you,' my older brother taunts,

chasing me down the hall.

I run to my room.

'You're not allowed in my room!'

I protest indignantly.

Sitting on my bed until he gives up.

The boys can't take a step over the doorway for fear

of the strap.

I feel safe there.

'You can't stay in there forever.'

'Longer than you'll wait,' I say, opening a chapter book.

I love reading.

Escaping to another place, another time.

I like my new school too. The freedom of biking alone.

Along friendly streets

with big old trees bowing over pavements,

providing shade.

They know me and I know them.

We're connected too.

Mum works long hours and I babysit.

Sometimes I even take time off school to do it.

I do the vacuuming and tidy and feel grown up.

We're not allowed in Mum's room either.

It feels weird when Morris tells me to go in.

I'm worried when he shuts the door.

It turns out Mum's bedroom isn't a safe place,

unless she's home.

I thought he was supposed to look after me,

but now I know different.

I pray he'll stop.

God, I'm yelling at you to help me.

I don't blame you.

I just don't understand.

If God is everywhere, he must be watching this.

Watching and doing nothing.

I can't figure it out. God answered my prayers before.

Why doesn't he do something now?

I'm desperate for help.

I'm screaming and crying inside my head.

God where are you?

Please help me.

I need someone to save me.

I think I might go crazy just thinking about it.

I drift outside myself.

Now it's not me it's happening to.

It's some other person.

That's better.

Now it's easier to cope.

I'm trying to figure out why he doesn't,

get caught.

A mysterious disappearance would work,

Or even a genuine 'sorry-I-won't-do-it-again'.

I keep talking to God in my head.

He's with me somehow, I know that.

Even though I can't feel him right now.

All my feelings are bad.

I'm outside my body looking down.

Some poor girl has a man leaning over her.

She looks dead.

When it's over and I'm curled in my bed, I keep talking
to God.

I still don't have the words, even though

I'm eleven now,

I know God must know and understand

my feelings.

The Bible says he's on my side, and I believe it.

I don't understand why he doesn't send someone
to help.

Maybe, he told them to,

and they didn't listen.

I've finally reached 600.

It turns out there is a marker.

I didn't see it at first.

It tells me I've reached the six hundredth step.

I wonder if there's supposed to be a marker for each hundred
after all.

Maybe I missed them because I wasn't really looking.

Too busy puffing and remembering.

At least I know I'm over halfway.

Seven hundred and fifty doesn't seem that far from
six hundred.

Then I'll be three-quarters of the way to the top.

I wish my thoughts would shut up.

Overthinking again.

Even trying to keep my days busy, they sneak in
sometimes.

Like now.

I don't want to relive all the horrible memories.

Sometimes they just won't stop tumbling over
one another.

Sometimes I can't stop wondering,

if I should have done something different.

I just want peace.

Isolated by my silence.

It happens over and over.

Morris takes me places now.

Into the forest,

beside the river,

the back of his old Land Rover.

I tremble each time I'm alone with him.

Dreading it.

He threatens me not to tell.

Says it's his right,

my education.

Not the kind that I want.

I'm still only twelve but I don't feel like a child anymore.

I don't feel innocent.

I know stuff I shouldn't.

I'm not ready for these strange sensations.

Mum frowns at me when he cuddles me.

Like it's my fault.

I stare with pleading eyes, hoping she'll step in,

take my place.

Hoping she'll say something.

She doesn't.

I'm too ashamed to tell her.

If I say something, everything will change.

Maybe for the worse.

But I don't want it to stay the same either.

There's a monster under my bed.

It's been there a while.

    Waiting to grab my ankles in the dark.

      At least that's what I imagine.

I need to go to the toilet.

    Can't wait for the morning,

      and can't turn the light on

        because it'll wake my sister.

Usually leaping from the bed

    and making a run for it works.

      Avoiding it.

        Not this time.

I will not run.

Tonight, I've decided to defeat this monster.

    To make myself strong.

    So now I'm sitting on the edge of my bed staring

into the dark.

    Telling myself there's no need to fear.

    Procrastinating and

      building courage

enough to resist.

I lower my ankles,

slowly,

and place my feet on the floor.

Heart pounding,

breathing deep.

Telling myself

it's only in my imagination.

Learning how to be brave.

Testing myself, controlling my thoughts.

For long moments I wait,

pushing my feet down into the carpet,

to stop from whipping them back up.

There's no monster under there.

I've beaten it with my mind.

I find strength,

for another time.

In preparation for the monster,

in the bedroom next to mine.

Arm around my mother.

Keeping her quiet.

I'm beginning to see a hero in me.

I'm thirteen now.

'You've got a bike, why don't you use it?' my brother asks.

'I like walking better,' I say.

    It takes longer to get home.

Morris says he'll take me to school today.

I know what that means.

I don't want to go with him,

    but I'm not allowed to argue about it.

'Can we take the boys too?' I ask.

    'They've already left,' he says.

      He sent them away.

He drives to the forest,

    and I become the lying dead,

      willing myself not to move.

      Not to feel.

I hate how my body betrays me,

    so I abandon it again,

      and my mind goes somewhere else.

Now we're on the way to school.

My floating mind re-joins my zombie body at some stage
on the way.

'Why don't you stop me?' he asks.

I stare ahead, shocked.

Unaware that I could.

Annoyed he's putting it on me.

'You like it, don't you?' he taunts.

The trees flick past the window, and we go over
the bridge.

Across the river.

A feeling of disgust washes over me.

I wish he'd just

drive off the bridge.

Let the water take him while I survive.

Arriving at school, I shakily get out of the vehicle.

Head down, avoiding him.

Feeling the shame.

As I move past his window, he leans over to gloat.

'I can make you pregnant if I want,' he says.

I keep walking.

Feeling sick at his words.

He has all the control because no one is stopping him.

The school building feels safe,

but now I'm worried.

Will he try?

I've been getting my period for over two years now.

Even though I'm only thirteen.

Early for a skinny white girl.

It's possible.

He could do it.

What if I did get pregnant?

The thought terrifies me.

I'm nearly at class when my brain clicks open.

It's like a lightning bolt sears my mind,

and makes the haze clear.

Something is very wrong.

Insight dawns.

Like scales falling off my eyes

I'm no longer blind.

What he's been doing is all wrong.

It's bad.

He's bad.

What I think next is an epiphany.

I. Don't. Have. To. Let. Him.

Don't have to go with him.

Don't have to.

Don't have to be chained by him.

'No' is an option.

I can be brave.

Stand up to him.

Stand up for myself.

I don't have to let him.

I've decided to stand up for myself.

Stepping out of the bathroom, I see him,

walking towards me with that look.

I know what he wants.

I stop and raise my chin.

He reaches out.

I back off and glare.

He steps closer.

'No more,' I say firmly.

Steel in my voice, cold determination in my eyes.

Anger warms me.

Ready to yell if I must.

Even scream.

Heart pounding, lips thin, chin high.

He stops, eyebrows raised,

throwing a cold blue glare at me.

Then he slimes to his room

and slams the door.

Stumbling down the hall and into the sun,

I let out the breath I'd been holding and gasp for air.

I'm shaking, but it worked.

This brave girl has a victory.

It's a relief,

       but elation does not come.

If that's all it took for it to be over...

         ...why couldn't I do that sooner?

It's over but not forgotten.

You have burned a wound,

on my soul.

Who can I trust now?

How can I be whole?

I search for a safe harbour,

Peace and unconditional love.

Where can I find it?

Only above.

Distracted by the sign.

It says, '700 steps'.

I don't realise the rock is loose.

My weight is more than it can take.

The sand moves, the rock wobbles.

I fall hard,

pain lancing up my arm as I try to catch myself.

Rolling down steps,

right knee and shin

connecting

with

one

edge

then another.

I groan and lie where I land for a moment.

Hoping I don't fall any further.

Amazed I didn't knock myself out.

Heart thumping.

Listening to my body for aches,

and breaks.

I flex my arms on the gravel,

    then slowly raise my aching body to sit on the step.

Distracted by the pain of now.

    Heart hammering.

My hand is grazed,

    my shorts are torn,

        and my knee is skinned.

Little pieces of gravel and dirt stick in the blood.

    More blood is starting to trickle down my leg.

I taste blood in my mouth as well.

That's when the pain registers.

Tears tug at my eyes,

    at the injustice of it all.

I indulge myself by holding the pain close,

    dwelling on my misfortune.

   But it does no good.

    Misery grows and

    taunts me

    with words of victimhood.

      Catching me for a time.

  Life is so unfair.

    Don't I know it.

Why did this happen?

On top of everything else.

Can't I just walk up some stairs,

without bad stuff happening?

I look at the blood and a tear mingles with it,

until my trembling hand covers the wound

with the sleeve of my top.

Like my other wounds – all covered up.

This wound bleeds on the outside though.

It hurts.

I stand on shaking legs, then flex my knee as the blood drips.

It still works ok.

Tempted to go back down,

and forget about my goal.

I look up and down.

Diversion is tricky.

I don't want to be a quitter.

My aim was the top so that's where I'll go.

I must continue to be strong.

It's probably just stubbornness.

Rebellion against giving in.

But it's keeping me moving forward.

High school was ok.

For me, it's not a total horror story like for some.

I'm good at it.

The studying and learning is interesting.

Knowledge builds confidence.

Prizes, good marks, music groups, drama productions.

The sanctuary of the library.

Get lost in belonging and achieving.

Keeping busy.

There's a lot of good times.

I have some great friends.

Youth Group.

Keeping busy. Focus on other stuff.

Morris leaves me alone now,

but

I don't want to be in the same house as him.

He disgusts me.

Rage simmers and randomly erupts into tears.

I'm angry, and fragile.

It's not like I have choices though.

Where else would I go at fourteen, fifteen, sixteen?

So, I keep the peace and get on with it,

dreaming about freedom.

I read a lot, come home from school late, go for long runs.

Shut myself off.

I want to tell someone about it,

but I don't know who and what would happen.

I talk to God about it instead.

A lot.

I'm pretty sure that's all that's keeping me sane.

When I'm not losing it.

It's normal for sixteen-year-olds to be a hormonal mess.

Right?

Seething on the inside,

then crying for no reason.

Tenuously trying to keep everything together.

Desperate for comfort.

Too aware of sex.

Attracted to boys, but suspicious.

Longing to be held,

but too scared to let anyone too close,

in case of, you know what.

One night, a friend walks past me too close.

His hand brushes my bottom.

'Don't touch me!' I yell at him.

He steps back, hands and eyebrows raised in shock.

My face heats.

He calls me out on it.

'What's up with you?'

I hang my head. *So many things.*

'Nothing,' I say.

'What?' he asks. 'You can tell me.'

I want to, but I can't find the words.

The feelings are too big and raw.

I feel sick at the thought

of exposing my shame.

My silence is a lie,

but I can't help it.

It's such a private thing, and I don't trust his response.

'I'm just having trouble at home, that's all. I'll deal with it.'

'Yeah, me too,' he says.

He hangs his head, and I see my pain mirrored

in his face.

I wonder if we both should say.

If it would make it worse or better.

What would happen.

It's hard to stay in control, to be strong and brave.

When I'm so fragile.

I'm with my friends.

We're having hot chocolate and talking.

About nothing.

A fly emerges at the end of my last gulp,

big and black at the bottom of the mug.

Sitting still, not floating.

I peer at it.

That's when I hear the tittering.

It's a joke mug.

I laugh and everyone else does too. It's a good gag.

I don't know when my laughing turns hysterical.

Suddenly I'm crying,

I can't stop.

I stumble out, wiping the string from my nose.

Humiliated that my pain has been seen.

Desperately pushing the panic down,

and scared at how close to crazy I am.

I want to scream,

But I might   shatter.

Beginning to hate him.

I thought you could be a father to us.

Make us a whole family.

But you were broken when we got you.

A selfish manipulator.

What happened to you and what is in that head of yours

to make you act like this

with no care for the consequences?

You damaged us –

drove a wedge between us.

A heart breaker.

Coward.

You stole from me.

You stole from us all.

Reading to heal, reading to escape.

I hide my swirling emotions in books.

They transport me to

different times and places.

Attracting my focus to other people's lives

and spaces,

away from my own thoughts.

The library has books,

about abuse and incest.

I discover I'm a member of a large group.

I begin to understand.

I'm not alone.

Not at all.

It's so sad.

For months and months and years,

books and more books –

child abuse, child development,

psychology, and theology.

Self-help, guidance.

About dealing with irregular people.

My bible now has notes in the margins,

    especially the verses about justice,

      reconciliation,

        and forgiveness.

I read and read.

    I take notes,

      write poems, start a journal, pray.

    It helps.

God is somewhere in the middle of the mess.

      The mess of this broken world.

I can feel him around me.

    With me.

    Slowly healing a bit at a time.

Service is also my saviour.

    By helping others, I help myself.

    I have friends, a purpose, a value.

      I soak it all up.

        It's not just me – it's all of us together.

The youth group leader took me aside one day.

She looked me straight in the eye.

No mucking around.

'One of the things I love about you,'

she said,

'is you always bounce back.'

She paused and eyeballed me

like she wanted me to know something important

without actually saying it.

There was a big semi-awkward pause before she continued.

'Bad things happen, and life isn't fair.

Some days are a struggle, and I see that you struggle,

then you just seem to bounce back.

It's a gift.

One minute you look like

the weight of the world is on your shoulders.

Then it's like a light goes on in your eyes

and that smile of yours appears,

and I know you'll be ok.

God has a plan for you.'

I wondered what made her say that.

What did she know?

Whatever the prompt,

it was healing. A relief.

I was seen.

I was heard.

I thought I might talk to her about what happened,

because maybe she knew something.

But I don't want to

open the wound.

Her words were powerful though.

They gave me space to move on.

To be more than what happened.

To talk about feelings if I needed.

But more than that –

I now had permission to keep bouncing back.

To be happy.

I'm out of town on a course.

It's nice to be somewhere else and learning new things.

Seventeen and just finished school.

Feeling significant.

Feeling grown up and at the start of my life.

I'm full of hope for a great future.

I want to make a difference and be a teacher.

Teach girls how to succeed,

how to think and grow strong.

How to make a future and to have hope.

I'm halfway through my practice at being a real teacher.

Living independently and imagining.

That's when I get the phone call from Mum.

'We're moving to Australia,' she says.

'Leaving in two weeks' time,

you need to come back now,

pack up your stuff,

and find somewhere to live.'

'But my course hasn't finished.'

'Come back now and pack your stuff or I'll bin it.'

'Where will I live?'

'I don't know, call your friends.'

'What about the others?' I ask.

'Sean's got a job on a farm,' she says.

'He'll be looked after with a room and board.

The other two are coming with us.'

I'm in a daze.

I'm not invited. I'm sad but relieved.

I don't care about Morris.

He can get lost.

But Sean's only 15, my sister is 7.

We're splitting up.

The decision has been made.

There's nothing to say.

My life is changing again.

I leave my course early,

go home,

and pack up my stuff.

I move into a friend's shed.

I'm alone now with no family.

They deserted me. Left me to fend for myself.

Feeling abandoned, but also,

Free.

The marker says 800 steps.

It tells me the number,

but I still doubt it.

I don't really care anymore if it's right or not.

It's just a distraction.

It only serves to tell me how many more steps,

that I must puff up.

Me pushing myself.

Ignoring the feelings and

focussing on fact.

My mind has gone numb.

My leg is still throbbing.

Misery circles me, but determination is at my core.

I stop thinking altogether.

Like a zombie.

I should have brought water.

I start to build a new life.

A job.

A new church in the city.

I immerse myself in serving.

A sense of belonging grows.

Achievement.

Focussing on the needs of others

means I'm not worrying about myself.

I soak in the sermons and discussions about

faith and life.

I have friends I respect.

Friends who are safe.

A purpose and a place

and Joshua.

He's my special person.

My future, my family.

'Let's not get into the physical stuff,' he says.

'It's too tempting if we start –

it's a sacred thing.'

It. Is. A. Sacred. Thing.

He makes me feel safe.

I trust him and start melting my heart.

He's protecting me, but

I also want to be held and treated tenderly.

To feel loved.

To know that it won't lead to anything else.

I want to hold him and keep him close forever.

I cling to him because I need him.

My heart's all in.

At nineteen, I imagine our life together.

A simple life full of love and service.

A purpose.

A hope.

A future.

After eighteen months together

He comes around for a date.

Except it isn't.

We aren't going out or staying in,

he's leaving me and

breaking

my

softened

trusting

fragile

heart.

I can hardly believe what I'm hearing.

'We're going in different directions,' he says.

'No, we're not.'

'I want to focus on my studies,' he says.

'I won't get in the way.'

'I think it's for the best,' he says.

I don't.

I don't understand it. I thought we were strong together.

I thought we were forever.

I thought you were my forever person.

Someone who would never let me down.

My mind goes numb. My eyes look down.

I feel like grabbing him and being hysterical.

Crying and begging and saying I need him.

Convincing him that our future is worth the work.

And the wait.

But I'm not like that.

I stare at him mutely, trying to

manage my feelings.

Trying to be strong.

I can tell he's made up his mind.

I wonder if I should try and change it.

But I surrender to the inevitable.

There's nothing to say to convince him.

No point begging.

No point screaming.

Too proud to cry even though I want to.

Please don't leave me. I need you. I love you.

'If that's what you want,' I say, hating myself.

It's not what I want, but

I'm not sticking up for myself.

Again.

I've already given him my fragile heart.

Already imagined our next five years and beyond.

Now what do I do

with the shell that is left?

My heart stays broken

while I wait and wait and wait for him to come back.

Hoping he'll see that he's made a mistake.

Hoping that he'll come back soon,

and we can get on

with being happy.

Things are different,

with everyone,

when Mum and Morris come back.

Like we're strangers somehow.

We're all in separate places.

Only little sister is still at home.

I visit on weekends to check on her.

Tell Morris I'll call the police if he touches her.

It makes me tremble to look at him.

To think of it happening again.

Not if I can help it.

I'll protect her if I can.

I visit to do another check – she's ten now.

'Where's your boyfriend?' Mum asks.

'We broke up,' I say, looking down.

Still fragile about my heart walking around

somewhere else.

He made the decision. There's nothing I can do.

I still love him.

I still want him back.

I still need him.

I'm still waiting for him to realise we're perfect

together.

'Push him away, did you?'

I glare at her.

If anything, I held him too tight.

'No.'

'It's a shame. I thought you'd get married.

You were always a cold fish, never wanting a hug.

Always pushing people away.'

I gulp and look away, willing the words to glide off me,

and not settle in my mind.

Then I feel angry.

I can't help myself and blurt it out.

'Maybe it's because of what Morris did to me!

Maybe I just need to feel safe

And in ... control!'

Anger-fuelled words, making me tremble.

I glare at her. Willing myself to be strong.

Trying not to cry.

Scared I'll get a slap.

Silence follows. It's out in the open.

I wait for the shock,

the denial.

'I told him to stop,' she whispers, head down.

'You KNEW?' I take a step back.

It's like a punch to the stomach.

'You knew and did NOTHING?'

I feel woozy and sick.

'We went to marriage counselling.'

My mouth opens,

but no words come.

Like a fish gulping out of water.

Suffocating in air.

Marriage counselling?

How does that help me?

Silence hangs between us.

'I love him,' she says pitifully.

Like that makes it acceptable.

There's nothing I can say that will make this better.

I stare at her stunned.

Hurt, betrayed.

She stares at the wall.

'Uncle Sid raped me once, and I never told,' she says.

It's her defence,

and criticism.

My eyes grow large.

My mouth goes dry.

She wishes I kept it unspoken.

'You knew and didn't help me…' I croak.

She shrugs.

'That's a woman's lot,' she says.

'It's what we have to endure.'

I stare at her dumbfounded.

Trying to process.

Trying to understand.

She's so wrong.

We should expect more.

Somehow, I feel older than my mother.

'Anyway, you've made enough trouble for my marriage.

I'm not going over it again.

Just drop it.'

She storms off.

Apparently, this is my fault.

I'm to blame for the troubles.

Marriage and otherwise.

Somehow, I make it to the car and drive home.

Zombie me

feeling betrayed all over again.

Hurt.

Blaming her.

Pitying her.

Understanding her.

900 steps done, only 100 to go.

I can't believe the top is finally so close.

My knee has stopped bleeding,

    but I feel worse inside.

The remembering is injury anew.

    The loss and rejection are still too fresh.

        The tears I've held back over the years,

        have hollowed

            a deep cavity within.

I wonder if the remaining pieces of my broken heart

    are turning to stone.

I grieve for Joshua.

    I grieve for my family.

        I grieve for me.

Morris left a note on the table for Mum
when he left.

Coward.

Good riddance.

You never were a real man.

Just a boy who only thinks of himself.

I feel sad for Mum's pain, and my sister's.

It was naïve to think the rest of us could be

a family again now though.

Whatever family is supposed to be.

We're all in different towns, different spaces.

I don't hear from anyone,

desperate as I am to belong.

No one wants to face it, so

I'm the scapegoat that ruined the family.

Like a needy refugee,

I cling to hope that I can get back in.

I try my best to make it happen.

I write to Sean over and over,

with no response.

Try to see my sister.

Phone my brother with no answer.

Invitations are ignored.

None are received.

The rejection stings deep.

I phone Mum one day.

'What's going on?' I ask.

'You know,' she replies.

'No, I don't,' I say. 'I don't have a clue. Why has everyone cut me off?'

Mum tuts.

Then there's silence.

I realise it's probably her doing. To save face.

She's blamed me and it works for everyone.

Especially as I've moved away.

'Don't you miss me at family gatherings?'

'Not really.'

'But I'm part of the family,' I say.

'Yeah, well, you're not wanted.'

My stomach drops to my shoes.

The air leaves my lungs.

My stupid mind can't fathom it.

I haven't done anything worthy of this scorn.

Drowning in the void,

my mind deflects the poison arrows,

then shuts off.

All I know is I want us to be a family united.

We all need it. Especially me.

I tried my hardest to keep everyone together.

I can't make them love me though.

Can't make anyone, not even Joshua,

my soulmate.

Can't force inclusion.

Even if family should be there no matter what.

It's not fair.

My knuckles go white as I grip the phone,

already hung up on the other end.

It happened to me.

I can't ignore it.

It's not the pain and loss I've suffered,

But what it did to me.

It's the rejection and betrayal

that hurts most.

I must transform what happened.

Mould it into an understanding for my future.

It takes time.

I can't be cynical for what might have been.

I can't be unforgiving.

For my own sake,

I must accept the challenges and tragedies,

not of my making,

and gather all the little pieces that plague me.

Make sense of them,

then put me together again.

And move on.

975 steps done apparently.

Only twenty-five steps to go.

A poster on my wall says,

      'We see things as we are'.

   I am broken,

      and sad,

         and so alone.

I need to belong, to matter.

I stare at the phone.

It's Mum.

'Hello?' I answer brightly.

'Your Grandfather's dead,' she says.

'He's being cremated on Saturday.'

I gasp.

'Where?'

'It doesn't matter, don't come.'

I stare unseeing at the wallpaper patterns,

as something suffocates me,

...I can't breathe.

'Why not?' I squeak. 'He was like a father to me.'

'Yes, well,' she pauses. 'It's best you don't come.

You're not welcome.'

I inhale sharply at the cut.

'Says who?'

Silence.

'I'm family,' I whimper. 'I need to say goodbye.'

'It'll make everyone feel uncomfortable.'

I wonder why,

then I wonder if it will or not.

I wonder what's been going around.

What everyone believes.

What terrible thing I'm supposed to have done,

and why no one is sticking up for me.

I wish someone would stick up for me.

Or talk to me about it.

It's easier to ignore me,

than confront what niggles at the edge

of knowledge.

Why do I care so much?

It would be easier on me if I didn't.

I'm tempted to turn up anyway.

The rebellious part of me fumes.

But it's not about me.

I don't want to make a scene.

Especially at a funeral.

Besides, I can't face it,

if it's true no one wants me.

The scapegoat released into the desert must not bleat.

It's pointless because

no one wants to hear.

'You can send something, and I'll put it on the coffin,' she's saying.

Whoop-de-doo.

Staring into space

after she hangs up,

I wonder if I should yell and scream and demand answers.

I'm not like that though.

Besides, I don't have the energy for anger.

I've already surrendered.

Maybe I'll never understand.

Tears well in my eyes and my shoulders slump.

I should just accept it.

I've been kicked out of the family for good.

Climbing into bed, I let grief overtake me.

Sobbing into my pillow until I'm all cried out,

wrung out,

like a limp rag.

I wake up feeling groggy.

My head aches from all the crying.

Nothing has changed overnight.

I still feel betrayed and rejected.

Numb.

My journal beckons.

I want to scream and throw things.

To force them to listen and acknowledge what has happened.

To hug me and say they're sorry,

That it's not my fault.

That I matter.

I want them to love me like they should.

Instead, it's easier to keep me out of sight.

Hide the shame.

Blame me.

After trying to keep my family together with my silence,

I've lost them anyway.

Maybe I should have said something back then.

When I was little.

I feel so rejected and alone.

Unwanted, unseen, unheard.

The house is deserted when I emerge from my written rant.

Typical when I need company.

Depression oozes into cracks.

It settles over me and in me.

Always me having to be strong,

because no one else will do it for me.

A robot dresses me.

Paralysed by the grey murk inside my head.

The pain inside my heart.

The same robot gets into the car and drives,

staring ahead unseeing.

I wonder what will happen,

if I cross the centreline

and drive into another vehicle,

or maybe a power pole,

or off a bridge   or a cliff.

Instead, I end up in the empty car park.

There's no one to smile at me when I need it.

Just a sign that points to the beginning of the

1000 steps.

And ends with 'Lovers' Leap'.

The last steps before the top emerge before me.

There's nowhere to hide from myself.

From the flashbacks

and memories

and trauma.

Each new stress picks at the scabs

of previous damage,

until the wound seeps its own tears –

enlarging the heart scars.

I'm tired of struggling.

Of being afraid of rejection,

of desperately wanting to belong

and being wary of everyone.

980 'Why do you attract so many boys? Stay away from them.'

982 'You're so proper, can't you just let loose for a change?'

984 'Hey sexy legs... come over here for a kiss.'

986 'You're frigid, such a tease.'

987 'We should go our separate ways.'

988 'You're not wanted.'

990 'You ruined my marriage.'

993 *'Why didn't you stop him?'*

996 'You'll make everyone uncomfortable if you come.'

998 'No, we don't miss you.'

1000   –   'You're not welcome.'

I've reached the top.

I stand at the clifftop, soul searching.

The cool wind whips my hair around.

It dries the sweat on my face and body,

cooling me.

An overwhelming sadness takes hold.

What's the point in living,

if no one cares.

I walk to the edge,

and look down at the tumultuous froth.

The powerful waves crash on the rocks below.

They're battered just like me.

Worn down.

Bleakness has overtaken my soul.

Like the clouds that have passed over the sun,

shading everything under them.

A shiver takes hold.

I wrap my arms around myself.

The drop is straight down.

'Never go right to the edge,' Grandad used to say.

'The ground could fall away,

and that'll be the end of you.'

The. End. Of.   Me.

Who am I anyway?

I look down at the drop.

It would be so easy to step over.

To be stupidly rash.

Impetuous about temporary feelings.

It's tempting, but

I'm not like that.

As much as I wonder about it sometimes.

I don't want it to be the end of me.

To give in.

I'm sad,

but it's just a selfish kind of feeling.

Feelings change.

I know my sadness won't last forever.

I have more living to do.

I take a big breath and fortify myself.

I turn my back on the drop,

and walk to my special place.

That's why I came, after all.

For.

Some.

Peace.

It's not the first time I've struggled.

It's not the first time I've come here.

This is my sanctuary.

Out of the wind.

Sheltered by trees. A cocoon in an alcove of bushes.

Pine comforts me.

The rough bark and

familiar scent of sap.

Big breaths, tree hugs, the vast views.

I go to my favourite spot and lean against solid,

then slide down to the earth.

Back against a trunk.

Anchored.

The soft grass and pine needles cushion my seat.

A wide span of sky spreads before me.

Stormy clouds, hints of blue.

Changing, moving.

The ocean stretches far and wide until it reaches the

horizon,

where the water kisses heaven.

Turbulent and powerful,

and calm.

I take another deep breath and enjoy the fragrance.

I feel so small here.

Compared to the universe.

Compared to the vastness of time.

I'm part of nature, a part of something bigger.

I sit still ... silent.

God is here in the quiet.

I am one with him

and the earth and sky and sea.

I stay still and stare.

To

gain

some

perspective.

To

breathe

in

peace.

The reason for the climb.

It's worth the effort.

It's beautiful.

I swipe at my eyes.

They keep leaking without permission.

It's what happens when your heart is squeezed.

My heart hurts.

My soul is wounded.

I'm covered in the shadow of others.

The struggle,

and heartbreak –

betrayal   and rejection.

I sniff, gaze at the horizon, and calm my breath.

God is here in the quiet.

Yes, there are bad times, but I'm with you.

Focus on all that is good.

Anxiety is chased away by gratefulness.

I watch as the wind chases the clouds to expose the sun,

and think about all the good things in my life.

So many good times mixed with the bad.

So much privilege.

Gratitude's soft melody gently lifts me.

I'm glad of the sun.

I'm grateful for the beauty of nature.

I have clothes, food, health.

The privilege of a free life.

The horizon glistens,

bathed in silver in the distance.

It's wonderful.

I wonder at the power and calmness.

How life goes on,

and how small my struggles are,

compared to others.

How short one life is,

compared to eternity.

Cherish each day as a gift.

Don't waste it feeling bad.

This too shall pass.

This day, these feelings, this life.

Choose to be happy. Choose to be kind to yourself.

My lens slowly changes as I wonder at the view.

A profound sense of appreciation grows inside me.

Life is amazing.

The birds sing to me.

Nature comforts

– its colour, fragrance and power.

I gaze at the storm clouds for a while,

moving in slow flight,

then seek the solace of closed lids

and sigh a thankful prayer.

Even clouds have a silver lining

and I'd rather dwell on that.

My knee is still throbbing, and my shin is swollen,

but peace grows.

Hope grows.

My tank is being filled.

I belong here.

I am one with the land, the sky, and the universe.

I was made, chosen.

I BELONG.

I have been and will be loved.

I can love.

I open my eyes when I sense shadow.

The clouds have covered the sun again,

   small as they are.

Compared to the sun, I mean.

  The wind whips my hair every which way.

 I push it away and look down.

A small mauve wildflower is nestled between two rocks,

  battered by the wind.

   It bends one way then the next.

I watch for ages.

  Its delicate beauty is mesmerizing.

Attacked by the persistent wind,

  surrounded by stoney ground,

   forced to grow strong.

    Triumphant as its head lifts.

You can be like that flower.

 Determined, resilient, beautiful.

The shadow is there only for a time.

Then suddenly the clouds part and the sun appears again.

It was there all along, of course.

Just hidden by something less.

The flower and I share a piece of it.

Feel it.

Bathe in it.

My face lifts to it with closed eyes.

I take a deep breath.

Rays of life and warmth inside me.

The ocean's smells floating around.

Inhale the scent.

Breath in, breath out.

The enemy is me.

The hero is me.

Breath in, breath out.

I am not alone.

Zombie mind and freezing heart thaw.

I bathe in the comfort of it.

I rest in the peace of it. Content.

I hear a noise and open my eyes.

A red-faced middle-aged woman is puffing towards me.

'Oh my,' she wheezes, brandishing a red first aid kit.

'Those steps are a challenge.

I had to stop so many times.

I like your wee hidey hole.

The sun is like a spotlight where you're

sitting.'

She drops the kit on the ground,

Bending with both hands on her knees.

Large gasping breaths consume her focus.

I watch as she gains control of her breathing.

She offers an open smile amidst big gulps of air.

'I saw you fall,' she huffs.

'Went back to car ... first aid kit... took ages... not fit...

at... all.'

She wipes the sweat off her forehead.

'Oh,' I reply.

My voice sounds strange to my ears.

'Would you like me to clean it up for you?' she asks,

looking at my bloody leg.

My eyes narrow at her.

No, don't touch me.

I don't need anyone.

I can do it myself.

I feel safe when I'm in control.

I take a deep breath.

Stronger together.

She's looking expectantly at me.

'Ok, thanks.'

'Righto, good,' she smiles, like she'd won the lottery.

I realise accepting her offer is not only a gift for me,

but to her.

'I'm Trish, by the way.'

'Amy.'

It stings but

Trish is efficient.

She uses a water bottle and gently wipes the blood

off.

I gaze at the moving clouds as she does it.

'You're brave,' Trish comments as she dabs antiseptic cream.

'You fell, but you got right back up again and

carried on.'

I grunt. Not only about the sting.

Soon the scrape is cleaned, and a bandage is on.

I feel much better,

and it's not just the bandage.

My knee still hurts.

'Thank you, Trish.'

I smile at her, and it feels good.

'Yes, well, we all need a bit of kindness,' she replies.

'Life can be a challenge, but I find that,

with gratitude, optimism is sustainable.'

I nod. It's true.

Trish restores her first aid items into their red home.

'I mean, each day I look for something to appreciate,

and something to look forward to.

It helps me keep positive.'

She sits beside me and smiles, the epitome of cheerfulness.

I don't like it. It shows me up.

I like it, it lifts me up.

Amazing what a random act of kindness

and a smile can do.

We sit in silence for a while. The view consuming us both.

Her breathing returns to normal.

Then I hear a sigh.

The rain clouds have settled in.

'I'll walk back with you in case you need help,' she says.

That's my cue.

I make a move to get up.

My limbs are stiff.

Trish suddenly thrusts her hand down.

I don't want to, but I take it. Trish is amazingly strong.

'Righto, "hop-a-long".'

She laughs at her own joke.

We walk slowly towards a path.

It meanders through the native bush to the car park.

I follow.

We walk silently, looking at the beauty around us.

'When I saw you hurt yourself,

I knew I should help.'

'Thank you,' I reply.

'I'm impressed you kept going.'

I nod. It was worth it.

To keep going, I mean.

After a few more steps we come to a sign.

'Two kilometres to the car park,' Trish sighs.

'Do you think it is?'

Home at last.

I walk into the kitchen staunchly.

My guard is up.

Still fragile,

still working through it.

Always will be.

I know that feelings pass though.

I don't have to be ruled by them.

I can choose how to be.

I choose to be happy.

One of my flatmates is preparing dinner.

The other is sitting at the table watching.

Thankfully they're not huggers.

I'd probably dissolve into tears again.

'Aren't you a sight for sore eyes,' Sonja says.

'We wondered where you were.'

Ruth frowns at my bandaged leg and red-rimmed eyes.

'Are you alright?' she asks.

'Yeah, I fell down some steps...

...and

...I'm having some family troubles.'

Sonja rolls her eyes.

'Been there, done that,' she says.

'You can't live with them; you can't live without them!'

She laughs and nudges Ruth.

'Just forgive them and move on,' Ruth offers.

'Anyway, that's why you've got us!

We're your family now.'

I form a small smile and sit at my place at the table.

My place.

'Are you eating?' Sonja asks.

'Yes, please.' I'm starving.

A warm feeling settles in as we eat together and chat.

I belong. There is a place for me.

I am seen.

I am heard.

I matter.

I can keep going, and not just survive.

That night, my journal becomes a reminder for future rough days.

Everyone faces challenges.

I'm not special in that regard.

Today started as a bad day. I felt so beaten.

Cradling my pain like a victim consumed me.

Overthinking it.

Wallowing.

My sanctuary restored me.

I felt God – my comforter.

I was reminded not to focus on the negative.

The rejection, betrayal, hurt.

Troubles for only a brief time.

Acknowledge them yes, deal with them, definitely,

but then move on.

A positive lens is a better perspective for life.

Gratitude is better than anxiety or depression.

The gnaw of pain will happen more than once.

Each time the thorns grip my heart,

I will not let it   crush me,

But it must   invite me,

to overcome the roadblocks I construct for myself,

and those constructed by others.

There is a rock, always with me,

offering peace and healing.

I still believe.

There's still good in the world.

I can be that good for myself,   and for someone else.

I can forgive and move forward.

Deny the monsters in me any victory.

One day at a time.

One step at a time.

Author's Note

- 1 out of 4 girls in NZ may be sexually abused before they turn 16 years old. 90% of this abuse will be done by someone she knows, often a step-parent, and 70% will involve genital contact.
- 1 in 7 boys may be sexually abused by adulthood.
- Approximately 1 in 5 New Zealand women experience a serious sexual assault. For some women, this happens more than once.
- The 16 to 24-year-old age group is four times more likely to be sexually assaulted than any other age group.
- Victims of childhood sexual abuse are twice as likely as non-victims to experience personal violence later.

Incest can be wrapped up in confusing messages of love and family obligation. It is normal for survivors to experience a range of conflicting emotions – anger, sadness, anxiety, guilt, shame and even wanting to protect their perpetrator. Many do not speak about it for fear of rejection. This silence makes survivors feel isolated.

During a sexual assault, it is extremely common to freeze as the brain shuts down in shock, making it difficult to move, speak or think.

Even after the events, it is difficult to put the situation into words. A sense of insecurity means victims don't know who to tell and whether to risk it. There is concern about whether the police will be involved, what will happen to the family, the risk of possible re-traumatisation, and a lack of trust about what support will be provided.

Therefore, only an estimated 10 out of 100 sexual abuse crimes are reported, and only 3 of those get to court. Sadly, only one of those is likely to get a conviction.

The trauma of sexual abuse plagues victims with nightmares, flashbacks, and unpleasant memories. It can lead to feelings of helplessness, self-blame, and anxiety. It is difficult for victims to trust others or themselves as they question their judgment and worth. Physical and mental health problems can continue to impact survivors as adults in the form of depression, anxiety, impaired interpersonal relationships, parenting difficulties, eating difficulties, and/or drug and alcohol misuse as a coping mechanism. The long-term effects have been correlated with almost every known mental health disorder and most of society's 'social problems' such as early teenage pregnancy, single parenting, and lifetime low socio-economic status.

Recovery
There is hope for victims of abuse. The single most important element in coping is confrontation. Silence is a predator's best friend, so victims need to take the unspoken and hold it up to the light with the help of a trusted support person.

Those who seek counselling are better equipped and resourced to heal from their experiences and are less likely to suffer from acute physical and mental health issues.

Recovering from sexual trauma takes time, and the healing process can be painful. With the right strategies and support, rebuilding a sense of control and resilience is possible. Forgiveness and healing are possible.

If you need help

If you're in danger now, call 111 or ask neighbours or friends to call.

Run outside and head for people. Scream for help so you can be heard.

In New Zealand, call the 24/7 Helpline on 0800 623 1700 if you are disclosing abuse for the first time, are a survivor of recent abuse, are dealing with the long-term effects of historical abuse, or are concerned that someone might be at risk.

You can also call 24/7:

Safe to talk 0800 044 334
Shine Helpline 0508 744 633
or Women's Refuge 0800 733 843

www.ingramcontent.com/pod-product-compliance
Lightning Source LLC
Chambersburg PA
CBHW050145110726

47898CB00008B/2671